AF207754

A Real Jack and Jill Story

Written by: Jill Heil

Illustrated by: Juniper Teffeteller

PUBLISHING
New York

Published by:
Aviva Publishing
Lake Placid, NY
518-523-1320
www.avivapubs.com

AVIVA
PUBLISHING
New York

Rescuing Jack and Jill
A Real Jack and Jill Story

Author: Jill Heil
Illustrator: Juniper Teffeteller
Editors: Brandy Thomas www.thomasediting.com
                     Leslie Helakoski www.helakoskibooks.com/critiques
Book Publishing Coach: Christine Gail www.christinegail.com
                     Patrick Snow www.patricksnow.com

Address all inquiries to: www.RescuingJackandJill.com

Published by:
Aviva Publishing
Lake Placid, NY
518-523-1320
www.avivapubs.com

ISBN#: 978-1-947937-81-9
Library of Congress Control Number: 2018911889

Rescuing Jack and Jill – Copyright © 2019
First Edition

Printed in the United States of America

Dedication

This book is dedicated to
my special little boy
"Happy Jack"

And to all of the other animals in this
world who deserve a chance at a good life!

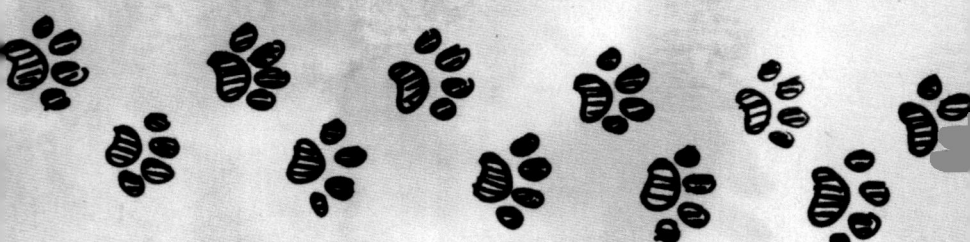

~ A Special Acknowledgment ~

My journey with my new furry friend Jack began at Clark County Humane Society in Neillsville, Wisconsin.

Clark County is a "No Kill" shelter and donations are the only resource for this facility to operate. All of Clark County's staff and volunteers work very hard to keep up with puppy mills and auctions, and also to help rescue animals that have lived in disgusting places. Jack came from a puppy mill auction.

I thank the team at Clark County Humane Society for spending their time, energy, and resources to help animals in this world!

Without Clark County Humane Society there would have been no Jack!

http://www.cchs-petshelter.org

A percentage of the proceeds of each book sold will be given directly to various rescue organizations.

A special thank you to my family and friends who have supported this passion of mine.

Rescuing Jack...

Hi, my name is Jill. I've always wanted a small white dog and I found him online. He was about four-years-old and looked very sad, most likely because he had lived in icky conditions at a puppy mill until the Clark County Humane Society rescued him.

This short story is about how I rescued Jack, my new best friend, and how we together rescued other dogs.

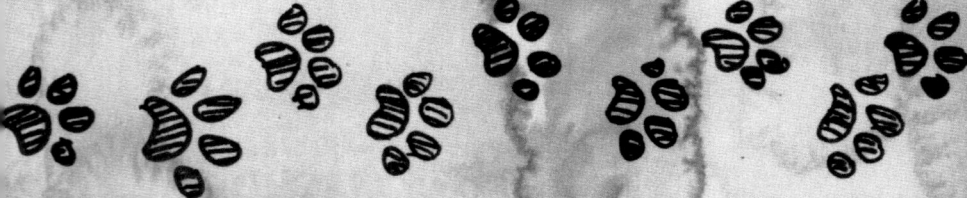

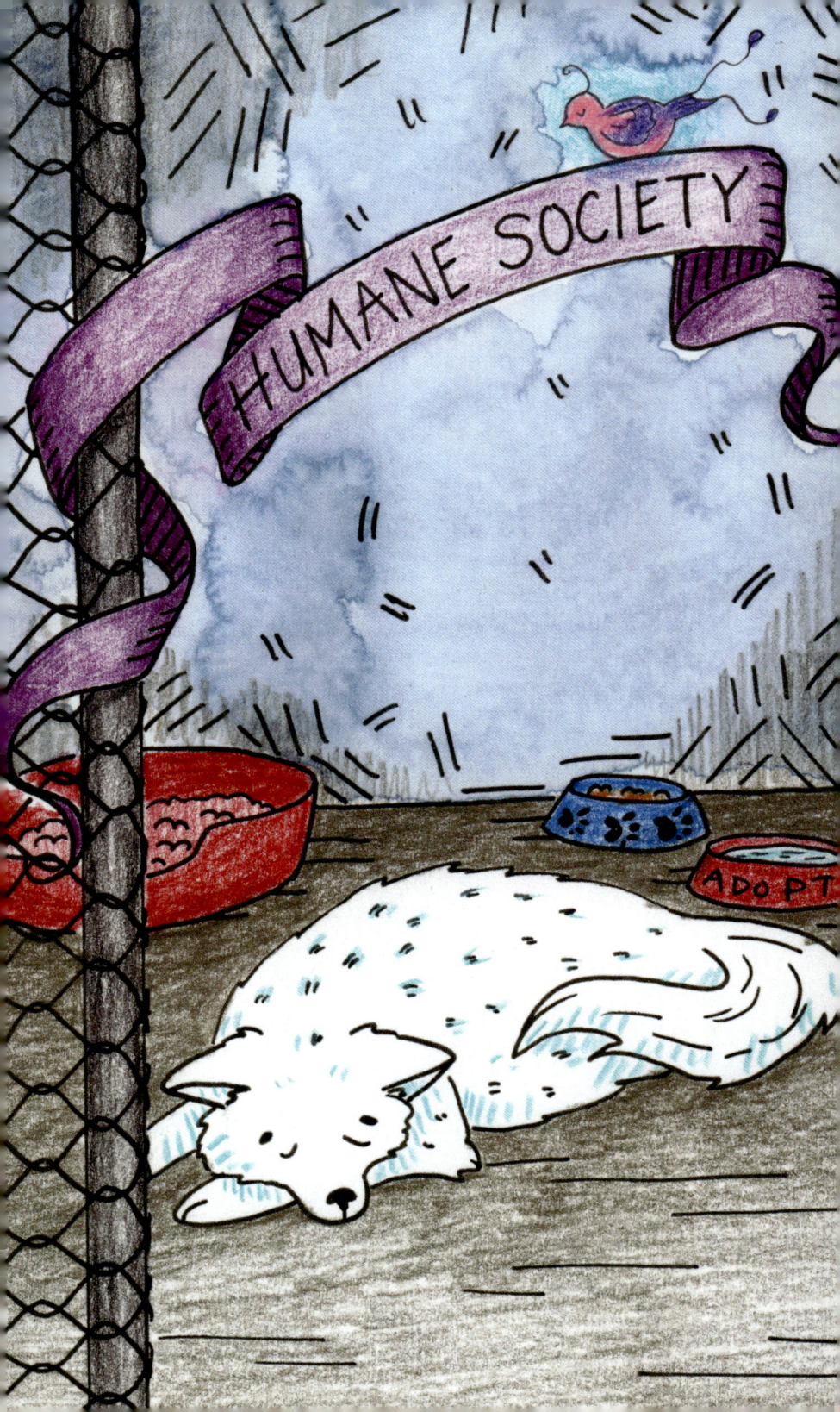

One Friday afternoon, I stopped at the dog shelter to meet him. A beautiful American Eskimo stared back at me, so sad and scared that he was shaking. I was super excited that he would be my new furry friend!

The next day, I was so excited that I wanted to hurry back to the shelter and officially adopt him. I put him in the back seat of my car and told my new pawed friend, "OKAY, your new name is JACK and I'm JILL and we're going to be a great team. Got it? YOUR new name is JACK!"

A couple miles down the road, Jack stood up and put, his little furry face right next to mine. As I looked in the rear-view mirror, I saw only his happy, funny face! Jack put his paw on my shoulder for the first hour-and-a-half of the three-hour ride home. Jack was so happy, he looked like he knew he had his freedom for the first time ever! With Jack's paw on my shoulder, I cried tears of joy for the first time. What a feeling!

A shy, and quiet dog at first, Jack stayed by the front door for a solid two weeks. I needed to build trust with him and teach him that being petted was a good thing. This was challenging because he was so shy. But, it's very important to build trust with a dog that comes from a puppy mill.

Jack quickly learned to walk on a leash, climb stairs, and use the bathroom outside. A smart little boy, he caught on fast.

Eventually, this happy little bundle of joy greeted me at the door, jumping up and down, every night when I came home!

Jack slept on the living room floor his first night. We both slept well because we were exhausted from our exciting adoption day. But not the next few nights! Jack cried all night long. I tried so many things to ease his fear; a teddy bear with a heartbeat, and even a kennel. But they didn't work!

Finally, exhausted one night, I just picked him up and put him on the bedroom floor, at the end of the bed. And guess what? We both slept really well! Jack just wanted to be in the same room with me at night!

Jack and I enjoyed lots of car rides. If I drove the car, my pawed kid came with me even on daily errands. The best part of Jack's day was a car ride, with the windows down and his hair in the air. We had many long trips to see family over the years.

When we traveled, Jack's protective instincts stood out. When anyone approached me or my vehicle, Jack would go crazy barking to deter them away from us. My furry bodyguard traveled with me as much as possible.

My protective instinct for him was a seat belt.

Jack loved winter. He could lay in the snow for hours, even when it was twenty degrees below zero with a wind chill of forty below.

Jack loved taking long walks in the snow and truly enjoyed his life in the wintertime. He especially enjoyed the backyard trail I made for him. When I looked out the window in the winter, all I saw was Happy Jack!

Jack never played with toys and, instead of interacting and playing with any of my friends, he preferred to just observe. Over the years, Jack found his voice and I thought he needed a quiet friend who would allow him to be Mr. Alpha Male. During an online search, I saw Hester, a blind reddish-brown Japanese Chin, who was marked "URGENT." I thought she could be good for Jack, as her profile reported that she was eleven-years-old, very shy and didn't bark at all.

I thought, Jack and I could provide a retirement home for older dogs to fill the rest of their days with as much love and joy as possible. Rescue dogs are the best! I had a meeting to see how Jack and Hester would get along. They were two peas in a pod; she was perfect for Jack, and he could be her big brother and help her! Next, the rescue lady came to my house to see whether it was safe for Hester. Because I have a fenced-in yard and a clean house, the rescue allowed me to adopt Hester.

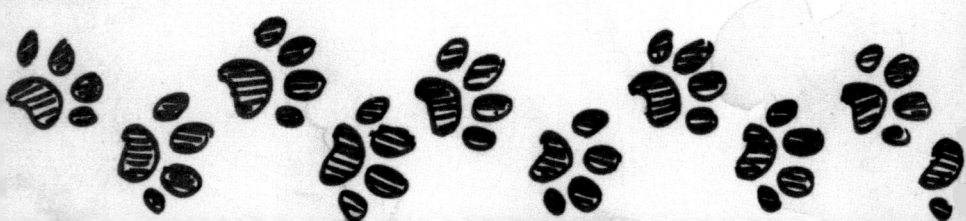

Hester needed a new name, so I changed it to "Precious Peanut" because she looked like a peanut. Jack relied on Peanut to get more of his favorite things: extra treats and more car rides. Jack convinced Peanut to beg for treats and car rides, and she was happy to help. They learned that it's all about the team work!

Peanut followed any noise in the house. So, with her keen hearing she heard more noises than Jack or me but didn't make any herself. I almost tripped over her daily! Peanut loved being on the couch with Jack and me. She was a quiet, shy little girl. I had eighteen fabulous months with her.

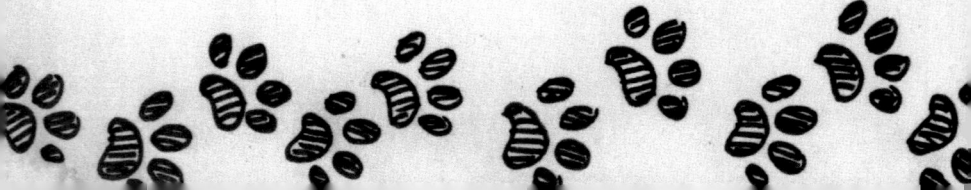

Months went by before I was ready to adopt another older dog. I found Possum, another Japanese Chin, online. After adopting her, I changed her name to "Little Miss Sweet Pea."

Sweet Pea was white with some caramel color. She was between ten and eleven-years-old. Sweet Pea always walked along the edge of the room. She was a delicate snuggle bug!

However, she also had a cough that led me to believe that she had only a few months left to live. I made them the best I could. One day, all three of us had our picture taken with Santa!

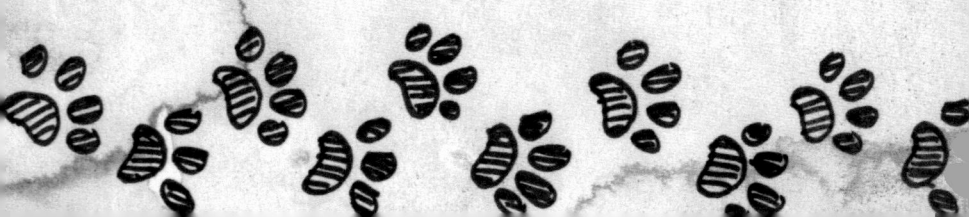

After Sweet Pea, the rescue lady dropped off a black-and-white, big-eyed Japanese Chin named Marbles, who was about ten-years-old. Her name suited her perfectly because she had giant eyeballs! After a week trial period, I adopted Marbles. She was funny, even the way she walked made me laugh.

When she used Jack as her pillow, he did not appreciate it! But, Marbles was quick to learn Jack's ways of telling her to leave him alone. He would get up, move, or growl at her. Marbles was so precious, funny, cute, and smart with such beautiful eye-balls! Marbles was a great companion for Jack and me, and I loved her!

After Marbles was called to doggie heaven, I adopted Izzi, a three or four-year-old stray. Izzi was very playful and happy and she loved toys and playing ball. Fetching tennis balls was Izzi's favorite game of all time. When we played ball, I laughed the entire time. She was such a good sport.

Izzi knew Jack ruled the house, and while she respected his authority, she had a funny personality with all people. My friends suffered from Izzi withdrawals after staying with us for the weekend. Izzi was the best snuggle bug in town!

Izzi always watched me come home from the front window and I laughed when I would see her excited face.

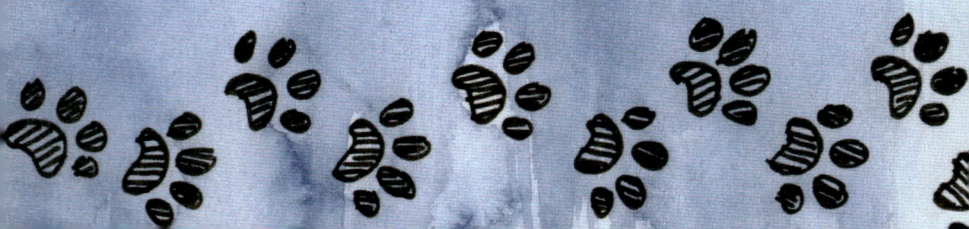

Just as people can have their differences, dogs can too. Jack and I worked with a local volunteer rescue and fostered a few dogs. Duchess, a seven-year-old blind and deaf dog, stands out. She loved human touch. She was a lot of work but, like all things that are hard work, so worth it.

Jack growled at Duchess anytime she got too close to him (even though she couldn't help it). Because she was deaf and blind, she struggled to understand that Jack wanted her to keep her distance. Because Jack never warmed up to her, I relocated her into another foster home. Not all dogs get along, just like people in this world.

A family with lots of love to share recently adopted her, so her story ends happily!

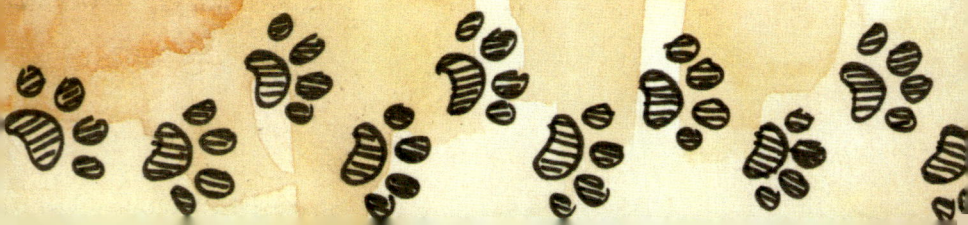

Once on a sunny but very cold, minus fourteen degree day, I drove to Iowa to take part in what is called a "Freedom Ride". I was to meet with people from a rescue organization. I drove a large van full of clean, empty crates and food for the rescue to use. I left with fifteen dogs, one to a crate, and each with his or her own little red blanket.

Oh! The smells! With fifteen dogs, an air fresher was called for. So I chuckled, rolled the windows down despite the cold and hoped for the best. The dogs quietly rode back to Minnesota. By the time all fifteen dogs were placed with their foster families the smell was gone. Each foster family gave the dogs a bath, food, and lots of love on their first night in Minnesota. I couldn't wait to do it again with Jack as my co-pilot!

Like all of the other dogs that have lived with Jack and me, Jack, at fifteen-years old, now needs a peaceful, happy place for his final senior days. He's getting older, moving slower and going blind. Oh, how I was going to miss Jack!! Jack rescued me over and over in our years together. When I was sad, he comforted me and gave me lots of hugs. Jack was easy to talk to, he didn't talk back, he just listened.

All of my furry friends have brought me so much joy. I have great memories from all of my furry housemates. And in the end, who rescued whom? I may have rescued them, but they rescued me right back. They turned my house into a lively home with lots of love and joyful laughter.

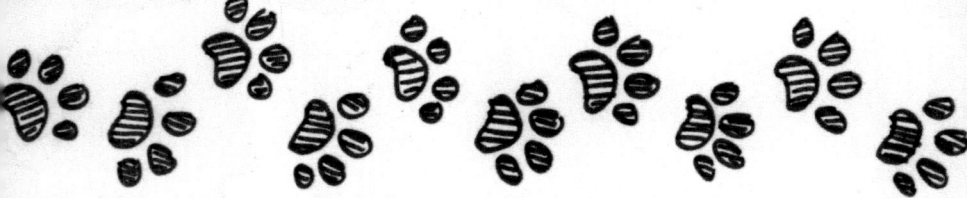

My friends, this is my real Jack and Jill story. My dog and I living the good life, while helping other senior furry friends find the love, joy, and peace they deserve.

A dog?

Just a dog?

NO.

Dog spelled backwards is. . .

The End

I would encourage you to visit your local Humane Society or rescue organizations, to rescue *your* favorite animal.

Please consider being a foster parent to help dogs or other animals in need.

Being a foster parent can be very rewarding, for you or your entire family!

www.petfinder.com
www.aspca.com
www.humanesociety.com

Having a dog in your home
is a great experience...
a bond unlike any other!

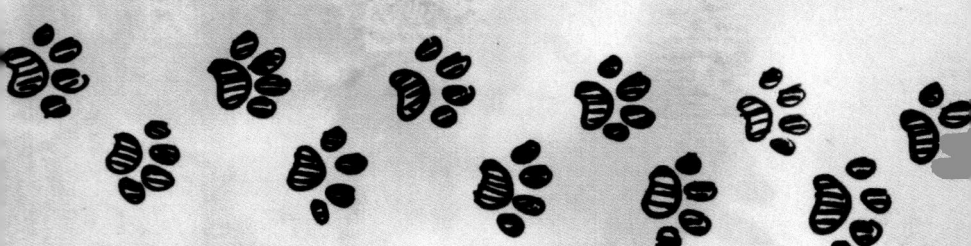

About the Author

Jill loves animals of all sizes and shapes. Jill started out with fish, birds, and house bunnies before adopting Jack. All of her pets over the years have had their picture taken with Santa for a Christmas card, which was enjoyed by all! Jill enjoys reading, music, basketball, hiking in nature, and the passing of the four seasons while residing in Minneapolis, Minnesota. Jill especially loves the freedom rides that help rescue organizations. All animals deserve a chance at a good life! Jill's favorite fortune cookie saying is: "Don't be pushed by your problems. Be led by your dreams!"

www.RescuingJackandJill.com

www.facebook.com/Rescuingjackandjill

About the Illustrator

Juniper Teffeteller is an artist based out of Knoxville, Tennessee and is currently studying printmaking at the University of Tennessee. She enjoys spending time in nature and with her cats, Pancake and Wednesday. More of her work can be found at:

www.sweetnepenthes.carbonmade.com

Jack